FIVE-MINUTE TALES

Kittens

p

CONTENTS

The NAUGHTY — Kitten —

Ginger was a naughty little kitten. He didn't always mean to be naughty, but somehow things just turned out that way.

"You really should be more careful," warned Mummy. But Ginger was too busy getting into trouble to listen.

One day, Ginger was in a particularly playful mood. First, he tried to play tag with his smallest sister – and chased her right up an old apple tree. It took Daddy all morning to get her down.

Then, Ginger dropped cream all over the dog's tail. The dog whirled round and round as he tried to lick it off. He got so dizzy that he fell right over. That really made Ginger laugh until his sides hurt.

After that, Ginger thought it would be fun to play hide-and-seek with the mice. He frightened them so much that they refused to come out of their hole for the rest of the day.

Then, Ginger crept up behind the rabbit and shouted, "HI!" The poor rabbit was so surprised that he fell head-first into his breakfast. Ginger thought he looked ever so funny covered in lettuce leaves. The rabbit was very cross.

For his next trick, Ginger knocked over a

wheelbarrow full of apples while he was trying to fly like a bird. He really couldn't help laughing when the apples knocked his little brother flying into the air.

And when one of the

apples splashed into the garden pond, Ginger decided
to go apple bobbing. How he laughed as the goldfish
bumped into each other in their hurry to get out of
his way.

Ginger laughed so much that, WHO-OO-AH! he
began to lose his balance. He stopped laughing as he
tried to stop himself falling into the pond. But,
SPLASH! it was no good – he fell right in.

"Help! I can't swim," wailed Ginger, splashing wildly around. But he needn't have worried, the water only reached up to his knees. "Yuck!" he moaned, squirting out a mouthful of water.

"Ha, ha, ha!" laughed the other kittens, who had come to see what the noise was about. And the dog and the rabbit soon joined in.

"You really should be more careful," said Mummy, trying not to smile.

"It's not funny," said Ginger. He gave the other animals a hard glare as Daddy pulled him out of the pond. But then he caught sight of his reflection in the water. He did look very funny. Soon he was laughing as loud as the others.

After that, Ginger tried hard not to be quite so naughty. And do you know what? He even succeeded ...some of the time!

— Where's —
WANDA?

S ally was worried. Wanda, her cat, was getting fat. She was behaving very strangely, too. She wouldn't go in her basket.

"She must be ill," Sally told her mummy. "Her tummy's all swollen, and she hasn't slept in her basket for days."

"Don't worry," said Mummy, giving Sally a hug. "If she's not better in the morning, we'll take her to the vet."

"Sssh!" whispered Sally. "You know how much Wanda hates the V-E-T." But it was too late, Wanda had already gone.

Sally and her mummy searched high and low but they couldn't find Wanda anywhere. She didn't even come running when they left out a saucer of milk.

Wanda was still missing the following morning.

"She must have heard us talking about the vet," said Sally, as they searched around the house.

They found all sorts of things they thought they had lost in the house, including Teddy, who was hiding under the sofa. But Wanda was nowhere to be seen.

"Perhaps she's hiding in the garden," said Sally.

They looked in the flowerbed, under the hedge, and up the tree. But all they found there were the birds.

"Sometimes she sunbathes in the vegetable patch," said Sally. But the only animal there was a fluffy rabbit.

"Wanda!" called Mummy, looking in the shed. Wanda often liked sleeping in there. But today all they found there were the mice.

"Maybe she's been locked in the garage," said Sally. So they found the keys and searched inside. They looked around the car. They looked in the car.

They even looked under the car. But all they found there were the spiders.

Wanda was nowhere around the house or garden, so Mummy took Sally to look in the park.

"Here, Wanda!" called Sally. But all they found there were dogs. Wanda hated dogs, so she wouldn't be there.

On the way home, they peeped over hedges and peered behind dustbins. Sally even sat on Mummy's shoulders so that she could look on top of people's garages and sheds. But Wanda was nowhere to be seen. She had disappeared.

"She must have run away," cried Sally. "We're never going to find her."

But Mummy had an idea. She helped Sally to draw some pictures of Wanda. Then they wrote MISSING and their telephone number on the pictures. They posted the leaflets through all the letterboxes in the street.

Later that afternoon, Sally and her mummy were sitting in the garden when Mrs Jones from next door popped her head over the hedge.

"Come and see what I've found in my laundry basket," smiled Mrs Jones.

Sally and her mummy rushed next door at once. When Sally saw what Mrs Jones had in her laundry basket she couldn't believe her eyes.

There, sitting amongst the washing, was Wanda. She looked very slim and very proud. And beside her

lay five tiny kittens. They were so young that their
eyes were still closed. Wanda hadn't been ill after all.
She'd been expecting kittens!

Mrs Jones said that they could keep the basket
until Wanda had finished with it. So Mummy carried
the new family home as Sally skipped beside her.

Sally was so excited. She just couldn't wait to tell
people how they'd gone searching for one cat and
found six!

— Fierce —
TIGER

Tiger wasn't really a tiger. He was a fierce stray kitten. People called him Tiger because he hissed and arched his back whenever they came near.

"You really should be nicer to people," said his friend Tibbles. "They're not so bad once you train them."

But Tiger didn't trust people. If they came too near, he would show his claws and even give them a scratch. That soon taught them not to mess with Tiger.

Tiger looked after himself. He didn't need anyone. At night he wandered the streets, searching dustbins for scraps and stealing food put out for pets. And during the day, he slept wherever he could – sometimes under a bush, sometimes on top of a garage, and sometimes under the cars in an old scrap yard.

One cold winter's night, Tiger was wandering the streets when it began to snow. He spotted an open window.

"Aha," thought Tiger. "I bet it's warm and dry in there." He jumped through the window and found himself in a dark porch.

"This will do," thought Tiger. So he curled into a ball

and was soon fast asleep. He was so comfortable that he slept all through the night.

When he finally woke up, there was no one around. But beside him was a bowl of food and a dish of water.

"Don't mind if I do," purred Tiger. He gobbled down the whole lot, then drank some water before leaving through the window again.

That day was colder than any Tiger had ever known, so when night fell and he saw the window open once more, he didn't hesitate to sneak in. This time, Tiger could see that the door from the porch was slightly ajar. He pushed it open and found himself in a warm kitchen. So he settled down and had a wonderful night's sleep.

When he awoke in the morning, he found a bowl of delicious fish and a dish of water beside him.

"Don't mind if I do," purred Tiger. And he wolfed down the fish and lapped up the water before leaving.

That night it was still snowing. Tiger returned once more. This time, when he went to settle himself beside the fire, he found a cosy basket there.

"Don't mind if I do," purred Tiger. And he crawled in and went to sleep. Tiger had never slept so well.

In the morning, Tiger was woken by a rattling sound. Someone was in the kitchen.

Tiger opened his left eye just a crack. A little boy was placing a bowl beside the basket.

Tiger opened his eyes and stared at the little boy. The little boy stared at Tiger. Tiger leapt to his feet and got ready to hiss and scratch.

"Good boy," whispered the little boy, gently.

Tiger looked at the bowl. It was full of milk. "Don't mind if I do," he purred, and he drank the lot.

After that, Tiger returned to the house every night. Before long, he never slept anywhere else. The little boy always gave him plenty to eat and drink. And in return, Tiger let the little boy stroke him and hold him on his lap.

One morning, Tiger was playing with the little boy in the garden, when his old friend Tibbles strolled past.

"Hello Tiger," meowed Tibbles. "I thought you didn't like people!"

"Oh," smiled Tiger, "they're okay once you've trained them."

Tiger was no longer a fierce stray kitten!

— A Home —
FOR ARCHIE

Archie, the black and white kitten, wasn't pleased. His owner, Tessa, hadn't given him his favourite fish for breakfast. All he had in his dish when he looked was some biscuits left over from the day before.

"Out you go," said Tessa, who was busy mopping the kitchen floor. And she pushed Archie out the door.

Now Archie was quite cross. He flicked his tail and swished his head. "I know when I'm not wanted," he thought. "I'll find someone who knows how to look after me!"

He jumped onto the garden fence and dropped into the neighbour's garden. Mrs Green always gave him a treat.

But as soon as his paws touched the ground, he heard a loud bark. Archie had forgotten about Bouncer, Mrs Green's playful new puppy.

Bouncer raced across the lawn and started to bounce around Archie.

"It's far too rough here," thought Archie, scrambling up a handy tree.

He jumped into the next garden. It belonged to Mr Reed. He didn't have a playful dog.

Archie strolled across the lawn and jumped up onto a window ledge. He was just about to squeeze through the open window, when he heard a squawk, followed by, "Who's a pretty boy?" Archie had forgotten about Mr Reed's parrot.

"It's far too noisy here," thought Archie. He made a quick escape through the hedge.

The next garden belonged to Granny Smith. She lived on her own and didn't have any pets.

"Meow!" called Archie. Granny Smith always had something nice to eat.

"Pussy!" cried a little voice from inside. Archie stopped in his tracks as he heard the patter of little feet running along the hall carpet. Oh, dear! Granny Smith's grandson was visiting. He always pulled Archie's tail. Archie decided to disappear before he got outside.

Archie squeezed through a broken panel in the fence. The next garden was rather overgrown. Some new people had just moved in and Archie hadn't met them yet. He hoped they liked kittens.

Archie strolled towards the house. He hadn't got far before he heard a hiss behind him. He turned around just in time to see a Siamese cat preparing to pounce. Archie, who knew better than to get in a fight with a Siamese, didn't stop to say hello. He flew through the grass, leapt onto the fence and run as fast as his paws would carry him.

"I don't think I'll bother going there again," thought Archie, when he stopped for breath. He sat on the fence and thought what to do next. As he sat there, a wonderful fish smell drifted past. Archie sniffed and followed his nose, his tail twitching at the thought of a wonderful fish breakfast.

Archie wandered past garden after garden where children screamed, birds squawked, dogs barked and cats wailed. At last his nose gave an extra big twitch. He stopped by a garden that was wonderfully quiet.

"Archie, there you are!" a voice called. It was Tessa. "I've finished cleaning, and I've got a lovely piece of fish for you!"

Archie purred. "Good old Tessa!" he thought. "She does know how to look after me, after all!"

Sleepy the
FARM KITTEN

Sleepy, the farm kitten, was always tired. He liked nothing better than sleeping all day long, and all through the night. While all the other kittens were busy chasing mice or scaring away birds, he was normally fast asleep.

"Looks too much like hard work to me," he'd yawn, before strolling off to find a comfy spot for a snooze.

One day, while the other kittens were chasing mice around the corn shed, Sleepy stretched and looked around for somewhere to nap.

"You can't sleep here," said the farmer's wife, sweeping Sleepy out of the kitchen with a broom. "Today's cleaning day and you'll just be in the way."

"You can't sleep here," clucked the hens, flapping him out of the chicken run. "We're laying eggs and we certainly don't want you watching."

"You can't sleep here," mooed the cows, shooing him out of the milking shed. "We're busy being milked, and a kitten can never be trusted around milk."

"You can't sleep here," said the farmer, pushing him out of the dairy. "We're making ice-cream and we don't want your hairs all over the place."

"I'm really tired," Sleepy complained to a passing mouse. "Can I sleep with you mice?"

"Don't be ridiculous," laughed the mouse. "Don't you know that kittens are supposed to chase mice?"

Just as Sleepy was about to give up hope of ever finding somewhere to sleep, he spotted the ideal bed. There was a soft bale of hay sitting on a trailer.

"Purrfect," he purred, curling into a sleepy ball. Within seconds, he was purring away in his sleep.

He was so comfortable, that he didn't even wake up when the tractor pulling the trailer chugged into life. And he still didn't wake up when the tractor and trailer bumped down the road leading to town.

It was only when the trailer shuddered to a halt that Sleepy woke with a start. He blinked his eyes sleepily, stretched, and looked around. Then he flew to his feet. He couldn't believe his eyes. He was at the market and the farmer was driving the trailer away with the tractor.

"Wait for me," meowed Sleepy, leaping down from the trailer. But the farmer had gone. "Looks like I'll have to walk all the way home," moaned

Sleepy, as he started to walk back towards the farm.

Sleepy walked all afternoon and all through the night. The cockerel was just beginning to crow the morning in when Sleepy finally made it back in through the farmyard gate.

"Hello, lazybones," called the other kittens when they saw him. "Where have you been sleeping all night while we've been chasing mice?"

But for once Sleepy really was tired. He was far too tired to explain where he had been all night. And it wasn't long before he was fast asleep!

— Shanty —
GOES TO SEA

S hanty, the harbour kitten, just loved fish. He ate every scrap that the fishermen threw away. And sometimes, when nobody was looking, he even helped himself to a few whole fish that should have gone to market.

"Don't you ever get tired of fish?" asked his friend Gull. But Shanty just shook his head and continued nibbling on a tasty sardine. He just couldn't get enough fish!

One day, Shanty had a brilliant idea. "There's only one thing that would be better than being a harbour kitten," he told Gull. "And that would be being a boat kitten. Then I could eat all the fish I wanted."

So the next morning, when none of the fishermen were looking, Shanty crept aboard the *Salty Sardine*, the biggest of all the fishing boats in the harbour. The sailors were so busy that they didn't notice the stowaway hidden beneath an old raincoat.

The sea was calm as the boat chugged out to sea, and Shanty had a great time dreaming about all the fish he was going to eat.

When the fishermen started pulling in the nets, Shanty couldn't believe his eyes. He was in kitten heaven. He'd never seen so many fish. There were mackerel. There were cod. There were haddock. And there were Shanty's favourite, sardines.

There were so many that nobody noticed when a few began to disappear under the old raincoat. And they didn't notice when the bones were thrown out the other side.

Shanty ate and ate, until he could eat no more. Then he curled up and settled down to sleep. But just as he was dozing off, something strange began to happen.

The *Salty Sardine* began to creak and moan. Then it began to sway and rock. Water sprayed over the sides as it bounced over the waves then crashed back down again. The *Salty Sardine* rode up and down the rough sea.

Shanty's head began to reel and his stomach began to roll. Oh, how he wished he hadn't eaten so many fish! Oh, how he wished he had stayed on dry land!

"We're going to drown," wailed Shanty, as a big wave crashed over him and the raincoat.

Soaked right through, Shanty peered out to see what the fishermen were doing. He couldn't believe his eyes. Instead of running about and screaming, they were carrying on with their work. One of them, who Shanty thought must be the captain, was even whistling. And another was eating a sausage roll. It seemed that for them, this was a normal day's work.

When the *Salty Sardine* finally got back to the harbour, Shanty couldn't get off fast enough.

"How is life as a boat kitten?" asked Gull, when he came visiting later that evening.

"Ah!" said Shanty, after he'd finished nibbling on a scrap of sardine. "Boats are all very well but give me the harbour any day. After all, how many fish can one kitten eat?"

Written by Gaby Goldsack
Illustrated by Alison Atkins
Language consultant: Betty Root
Design by Design Principals

This is a Parragon Book
This edition published in 2003

Parragon
Queen Street House
4 Queen Street
Bath BA1 1HE, UK

Printed in Spain

ISBN 0-75259-583-0

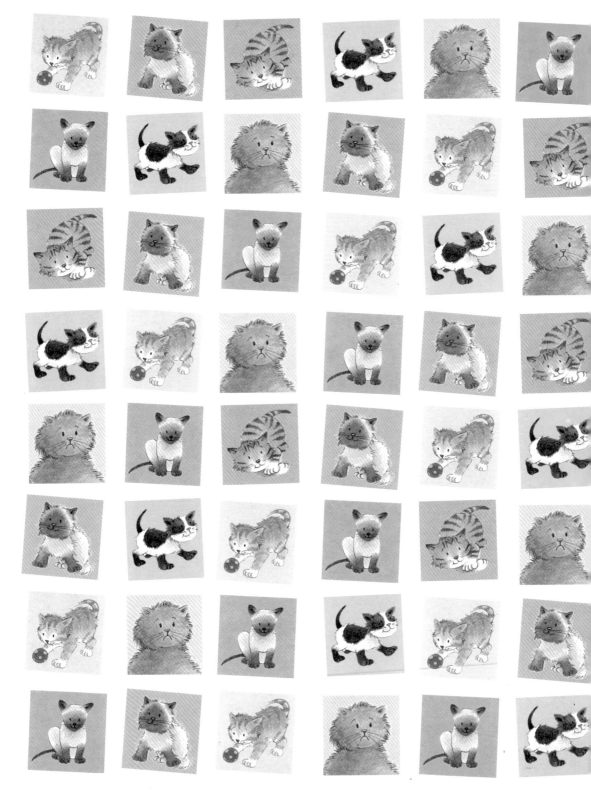